"I have been reading Ammiel Alcalay's striking novel *Islanders* with deepening pleasure and admiration. Readers eagerly anticipating the next breakthrough in American fiction need wait no longer. I can't begin to convey the excitement and sense of discovery as one plunges into Alcalay's gripping narrative. It's as if fiction were being written for the first time, or reinvented. One is reminded of the fierce interiority of Robert Creeley's *The Island*, of the hard-scrabble life depicted in Ed Dorn's equally innovative *By the Sound*, of the fitfully contained violence of Michael Rumaker's *Gringos and Other Stories*. But *Islanders* takes us beyond the work of these practitioners of the 'new American story.' There is an arresting obliquity in the telling, a more profound sense of story beyond the constrictive banalities of plot and character; though there is powerful narrative tension and the people are eminently alive, more vital than if they were merely made up. The coastal towns described are more intensely real in Alcalay's vision of his people's conflicted encounter with them than if they were simple way stations in their progress into desperate revelation. This is fiction that draws you into itself leaving you sadder and wiser at its conclusion. This is fiction that doesn't disappoint. *Islanders* is the real thing."
—Peter Anastas, author of the novel *Broken Trip* and a memoir *At the Cut*

"In *Islanders,* Ammiel Alcalay's subject is recovery of the past, not in nostalgic recollection but, through the careful articulation of detail, the redemption of it. And these details are mostly those of work, both its drudgery and those vivid encounters in which shared tasks reveal rich and varied qualities of human exchange. Each remembered event is treated with distanced respect, often almost as ritual. Each failing and loss is given its worth and dignity. *Islanders* is hypnotic, a work of tough poetic elegance and great beauty."—Toby Olson

"Ammiel Alcalay brings the ocean, its mist, boats, pontoons and islanders into a land-locked contemporary American literature. He sets his gaze on a particular bit of the world and lets that place unfold its kinetic essence in such a way that the novel is never finished but rather, it simply stops at a certain point, and then goes on beyond its pages in the reader's mind.

The narrator of *Islanders* is constantly adjusting his lens, focusing on scenes both 'real' and 'cinematic,' and that ambiguity keeps us riveted to the text. The reader gets caught in a flow of perceptions that become a meditation, a smooth continuity that mixes people, and their human passions, inextricably involved, with particular objects, so that one wonders: am I reading, seeing, or remembering? From one ordinary gesture to the next ordinary experience we reach a kind of an underwater state of bliss, which is constantly fleeting, like everyday life.

There is in Alcalay's work an unabashed tenderness for the world as it is, and that makes him courageous, different."—Etel Adnan, poet/writer

Islanders

Islanders

Ammiel Alcalay

City Lights Books • San Francisco

Cover and interior photos by Ammiel Alcalay
Cover and interior design by Linda Ronan

An excerpt of *Islanders* was published previously in *Damn the Caesars*.

Library of Congress Cataloging-in-Publication Data
Alcalay, Ammiel.
 Islanders / Ammiel Alcalay.
    p. cm.
 ISBN 978-0-87286-506-8
1. Self-realization—Fiction. I. Title.

 PS3601.L3426I85 2010
 813'.6—dc22

                            2009050500

Visit our website: www.citylights.com

City Lights Books are published at the City Lights Bookstore,
261 Columbus Aveneu, San Francisco, CA 94133

to Gilbert Sorrentino (1929-2006)
in good memory

I know that peace is soon coming,
and love of common object
— Edward Dorn

THE TABLE

He struggled to remember the table, a big table, unpainted, unstained, with simple legs, the whole thing cluttered with papers, objects. In the corners stacks leaned precariously, pens, pencils, scribbled notes surrounded by magazines, radio parts, half-used matchbooks. The table he had now was neat but his fingers picked and scratched at the damp label on the wet bottle that sat before him. Her arm stretched in front of her, then shot down past her mouth and the cigarette there as she spoke. "Five letters, they buried gasoline and shells and everything under the pyramids, each letter in Egypt stood for another stash."

The young man picked at the label. The woman spoke of her son, how he was privy to secret information, the day he left, her eyes looking past the bottles lined in rows before the dismal light that rose behind them, gazing at the water on another shore. How firm her skin was then, her waist thin where her full legs met as if rising further in a perfect X, her breasts held by a black satin cloth wrapped around and tied, the ends of the knot down her brown back swinging and waving as she walked. But that was a long time ago, when the railroad stopped right in front of the hotel, now just a figment in the imagination of the old or a faded photograph in the plate glass window of the barbershop. Her boy wore white from head to foot and she stood out against him as they walked arm in arm on the thin border of wet grass that led to the beach. She spoke to him as if she knew those last few dollars would last forever.

War of the Worlds, she heard *War of the Worlds* at the diner while she took an order from an older driver, his breakfast at night. Months and months already since she had smelled the wildflowers that grew up on the hill past the quarries, hundreds of pads filled with scribbled coffee, bacon, eggs, toast, jelly, jam — honey, an egg in my milkshake, ice in my coffee, sugar in my tea, you and me.

She went with them across the dark lot, the lights against the dull road accompanied by engines, shifting gears, a steady fog around the bend that led to the tunnel, beyond the dim apparition of buildings rising in a soft glow. They always showed her pictures of their kids and she knew their names as well as what they did. She walked home alone across the road to her bungalow by the marsh, lay in bed and watched the lights and shadows as they came through the thin curtains and ran across the ceiling. Word of marches came, and hordes of troops. The older drivers talked, the younger ones were eager, scared and eager.

"A bastard," she said as the young man looked up from his almost peeled bottle at the glowing orange tip that hung past her lips, "but smart, and they're the worst," she said, nodding in agreement with herself.

The young man thought to make a story of it,

the woman, the son she had, some years they lived, the things that happened around them, but he also kept thinking about the table, where it had been, and couldn't remember, the size of the room, what wall it leaned against and the things that lay on it. His day had been long, the streets hot, filled with other sweating bodies, his feet ached and names repeated themselves in his head. Two stories he had read years ago stuck to him, and as he looked at the bottle and the woman he thought about the men that wrote them, saw the men themselves, in long overcoats with cigarettes, hunched over coffee in some diner, their rooms, filled with smoke, crumpled papers, completely removed from what they were writing about, the people they wrote of never imagining they were being written about, the idea that someone was recording the facts of their lives, the circumstances they lived in.

～

As if it had meant nothing, he would stay away. Occupy himself. The city seemed almost enough. It was hard to believe there were people scared to walk in the city. And that there were, after all, only other people, walking. He sat one morning with a man on a corner, the man watching the traffic, he watching the man's lips slowly speaking of a daughter, a few lines in an obituary page, the grave never seen. The man's eyes, unused to being closed, hand holding a paper bag. There was work, always he'd heard, an honest day's pay for an honest day's work. Exactly where this had come from he never quite knew or bothered to find out. He never minded work, doing it with a sense of pride, that things could get done and he would be the one to do them. There were stories that people would read and say, why yes, this is very good, but that didn't really matter much, not as much as the turning out, of more. The constant work involved, the involvement, then. There were people who liked to see him for the stories he told, saying, yes, he's such a character, isn't he, and where on earth does he meet all those crazy friends of his. Others were more like brothers or sisters, with not that much between them that had to be said.

Somehow, though, nothing fit. The stories themselves, it was useless to fight. These things he felt. That when he wasn't with her there was an emptiness, a finality, desperate almost.

"It's hard to keep up tradition," he said, holding the flowers. "Nobody does it anymore."

"They're beautiful, they are," she said, smiling. And then there were those other flowers, her mother's face full of defeat, her tears freely on his shoulder as his, too, on hers.

∼

It seemed senseless to go to sleep as the sun rose. There were things last night he was supposed to do tomorrow that became impossible to even consider, now that tomorrow had already become today. So he would walk, maybe there would be work. The sun had just begun its ascent, the light hitting the buildings at peculiar angles making the bricks yellow, the fire escapes dance. The white paint on the front of the bar was thick and chipped, the age of it, its actual substance. He pushed open one of the swinging doors, struck for an instant by the darkness, the darkness of this place.

"Top of the morning, Cap.'"

"How goes it?"

"You know, the usual. And when there's a little extra . . ."

"That's about right."

They sat in silence for a minute or two before he asked: "Any work?"

"Well, I believe I might fit you in a little later."

"That's good, don't let anyone ever say you're not a scholar and a gentleman."

He stared out the window, the thoughts beginning with the silence, the staring out through the window, as if he was seeing doors, one after another, but never again, like before, just things reappearing. He held two fingers up to the bartender and kept staring out the window, the trucks roaring by, postmen beginning their day, the street coming to life, watching the sun, now bright, now shining, as the day became, through the window, whatever would become of it, he watched the day.

~

Artifacts, his own useless ones, or so it must have seemed to others. Newspaper clippings, matchbooks, pencils, pens with names of businesses on them, ashtrays, ticket stubs, a shoe horn, church keys, automobile leaflets. Even then, as a boy, there were great lengths he would go to in order to demonstrate something. Once, walking with a group of kids on a familiar street a strange boy stopped and pushed one of his group. He grabbed the strange one and, before he knew it, felt knuckles under an eye that stayed half shut as his head rested on the cool sidewalk. News traveled fast so she knew about it. The blow hadn't been quite enough to blacken the eye so the boy made it up with shoe polish that night so she would see him the next day even though she and everyone else knew it wasn't that bad. When he went in to adjust his disguise he couldn't get the stains off the sink in the boys' room. The knobs on the faucets had springs in them so the boys wouldn't leave them running and flood the sink, leave them on till the water topped and flowed down over the floors, running out the door and filling the halls, till the spigots rusted and the water froze and they could skate away from their assigned rooms, slide down the stairs and escape into the cold, fresh air. Consumed as he was by her, she never knew it, never knew of his elaborate schemes, each move and thought a signal toward some sort of consummation, the brushing of their hands, his hand on her hair or resting on her shoulder even if only for an instant. He never knew whom she loved or if she had loved anyone, whether anyone other than in their dreams had plunged toward her soft stomach, been consumed by her strong thighs or laid their head in her long round breasts. He had checked for flats that night, and swore to her that he heard the tires bump as he pulled over on a curve at the top of the hill by the ocean in the soft grassy bank under the bright moon. He walked slowly, checking each tire, bending to the road to inspect the wide white sidewalls, the light of the moon against the baby silver caps, a wave etched in, painted red, on which the outline of a ship crested, above that the word PLYMOUTH in small square letters. She laughed out the window as he got up from the grass and put his foot on the running board to reach in for her, the old blue car looking almost new in the moonlight reflecting off the ocean below. After that summer it sat in an empty field for many years. Once he had gone to look at it. Weeds had sprouted through the rotted floor and the little paint left was dull. Stuffing from the seats hung out of the rips and holes the sun and rain had made. Spiders inhabited the spaces between the rear window and the back of the seat. Only one tire had any air left in it and two of the windows were broken. The doors still clicked shut tight but the right one made the rear quarter panel flap since the support bolts had rusted off. The silver on the mirrors had peeled and spots of black shone through. Brittle leaves lay thick on the floor like on the path through the woods that led back to the old house, now boarded up since the new people had made it an early season. These mornings when he got up he wondered whether there would ever be other times like those they had together or whether he would even see her soon or in the distant future, the plan he continued formulating daily, of how to approach her, what to say, one plan if he saw her from a distance, another if they met unexpectedly. The tedium of his acts gained steadily on him and formed a great weight he carried with him, and though through the screen each morning the birds sang to him and him alone and the air brought him the taste of the sea to gently lift him out of his dreams and into his shoes, he still walked slowly and without apparent direction. Each morning he stumbled around the small rooms of the shack arranging things he had set in disorder the night before. Books and papers lay scattered in the bedroom, clothes thrown at random, the dishes still on the table and sometimes the radio still on. The cool air on their backs and their walk in the coarse chilled sand seemed vague to him now, a moment in a movie he might have seen as a child. He referred again and again to what seemed his last surviving hold, a vast catalog of references that she could never know the order of. Randomly, beginning at the end of the beach, working her way to the other end, she wanted to count the rocks jutting out of the water. Or ride a horse down the beach. A way to say what they wanted, whether in cars, or houses, a return to something they thought they might have had, her green eyes and cheeks full of sweet blood the day they had picked apples, the train rumbling by as they kept driving, further north, one looking out one window, another out the other (sometimes I wake up crying, she said, water hitting the windshield), dead leaves piled by the porch of a passing house, the shape known, some old form against the corner of the street, her return in the November sun. Return, as if such a word could even be considered, something so vague as misplaced memory, none ever offered, none saved.

∼

Lying in the singed grass of the empty field near the old rusty tractor all he could hear were the tall corn stalks swaying in a field he couldn't see. Far from the water wheel and the brook rushing over the rocks and hitting the spiles of the footbridge he abandoned himself to the breeze and the enormous day that stretched forever in a blend of light that didn't divide the shimmering whirlpool dying to be green from the already parched and dead. In the fall he died. Every fall he died, thrown into the dark pit, the lid suddenly closed tight over the sky, trapped in the black among raw sacks of grain, having killed the bird and knowing it was a sin, not having swam enough: neither a fish unable to emerge dry nor lost in the fathomless blue trying. On the empty road, passing the dilapidated clapboard houses whose once white sides were already long grey he thought of what he would tell them and fixed the design in his mind: opal wheels revolving in the night, unknown doors at the end of paths skirting the ocean, the descent whose access and issue only he knew. On damp grey mornings when they were marched out for their daily air against crumbling walls soaked with piss and scribbled arrows tenderly piercing broken hearts, he described his underwater caves, the sun that warmed him through the glittering aquamarine prism that enveloped and hid him, fearing nothing more than the sound of his teeth smashed into his palate as they hit the steel spout of the water fountain, propelled by an unexpected but constantly anticipated blow to the back of his head that hounded him like a lost brother: his brother perpetually waiting to slam him repeatedly back into the pit, to trap him in corners and suffocate him until the pattern of the floor or the dullness of the ceiling obliterated his tears, to chop and jab at his ribs and pound his back until he fell with the dull thud of slapped meat and felt his nose wet and the gritty taste of blood and dirt mixed into a thick coarse mass settle on his tongue.

$$\sim$$

The boy walked around with a ball of string. He showed the string to the two men who were working on an engine. The man looked at the string and the boy and told him to take it to the back of the garage and wrap up some boxes. The boy walked along the long driveway stepping over puddles and truck tires. There was a green truck with a wheel off in front of the garage. The motor was torn apart and lay in various sections and pieces underneath the truck, which was up on blocks. The boy looked at all the parts carefully, at the truck, and above him and to all sides at the tools and signs hanging on the walls. Toward the back there was an old coupe. The boy walked over to it and grabbed the door whose window was open and hoisted himself onto the running board.

Outside a little girl yelled for her mother. The boy turned and saw her through the dirty window sitting in a small plastic swimming pool. A dog was sprawled out on a tuft of grass beside the pool and every now and then the dog swished his tail to ward off a bothersome fly. A woman's head appeared out of the door at the top of the back stairs and told the girl to wait. She turned from the door to the table in front of the window, there were some sheets and a pillow on it. The baby looked straight at the ceiling past the woman's hands as she quickly picked the baby up by its bottom and slipped a diaper beneath it that she wrapped and pinned. Carrying the baby, she opened the back door and walked down the green steps into the yard. The little girl in the pool splashed water at the dog and laughed. The dog brought his head up close to the pool and looked at the girl who splashed him again. He shook his head, got up yawning and walked over to the farthest end of the yard where he scratched the ground and lay down under the shade of a tall tree.

The boy got inside the coupe and slid over behind the wheel. He put his arms on the wheel and though his feet couldn't reach the pedals he pretended he was driving. One of the men came into the back of the garage to get something out of one of the tool chests. He picked through the sliding red drawers and took out a few wrenches, some pliers, and a cold chisel.

"You're blocking traffic," yelled the boy from behind the wheel of the coupe.

The man laughed and walked over to the window of the coupe and stuck his head inside.

"Stop bothering the men, don't you see they're trying to work."

The boy's head snapped to his right and then

looked straight ahead through the windshield before letting it hang as he stared at the pedals he couldn't quite reach.

"It's no use, when I talk he doesn't listen."

The boy heard her step, first quickly and then slowly as she walked past the engine parts, then quickly again as she went out toward the driveway, his head coming up slowly as he stretched upward to watch the back of her move away in the tiny rearview mirror.

∽

He was taken to a place that was set at the bottom of a hill with a lot of windows and many doors. Streets led in all directions from where the place was to many rows of trees and houses. Every few years there was a different place he would be taken to and he would have to go there, almost the same as the place before except the new places got progressively bigger. As the places got bigger it got easier not to have to go, since the length of time needed to realize he wasn't present also increased due to the many more channels information such as this had to travel. The first place was easy. When they told him to count, and count to 100, he thought it was some kind of joke and as he took off his jacket and boots and shook off the snow he counted. For this a woman called Mrs. Cleveland gave him a gold star that she told him to lick and then stick on a piece of paper that had his name on it and hang it on the wall in the corner where her desk was. Then she would ask another to count. There was a place before this one that was below, a larger room with more children in it and no seats or desk but the floor. The name of the woman hadn't registered, although maybe then they weren't supposed to know or remember such a thing so maybe she was without a name. The names of the children didn't register either, the fence by the parking lot between the streets that led to the hills with trees and rows of houses, the tracks of the trolley and there on the corner the billboard (JOE & NEMO'S) and underneath the billboard was the building that had the diner with the stainless steel and booths lined in rows against one side by a large window where the older kids, sometimes boys sitting next to girls with their arms around each other, ran around or pounded the tables and threw water at each other. Joe would appear from behind the steam to take them to the door where they would knock on the window from the other side and makes faces at the others and Joe behind the steam. Afternoons passed like that or he walked by the tracks that curved then went straight for many blocks before curving again down a small hill where he lived. There was a garage door on his street with a box outlined on it against which he pitched a tennis ball, the whole game from beginning to end, nine innings or if it went extra he even relieved himself in tight spots as the crowd observed his every motion on the mound, the way his head touched his cap as his feet dug the dirt by the rubber and he'd pick up the resin bag, drop it, and turn the ball over and over in his glove before pitching. Over and over he repeated the motions and received the signal till dark and tired, the game over and the crowd gone, he'd sit alone by the fence and look at the patterns in the cracked cement, feel the air become a breeze and watch the sky return to darkness.

~

A slow steady drone proceeds at intervals, stops then starts. One tall and one short man lean against a door. Their eyes follow the moves of two who sit some distance from them, their words lost in the machinery. All see the blind man tap his way along with his coins chattering in his cup, some lean toward, others away, images played in the mind, reminder of another place or scent of hair or exact sway of a body receding in the distance down a long steep hill. Beyond the weeds her figure, clad in a light blue skirt with an anchor of deep blue sewn to her chest, sits behind pails and sand boxed in by a decaying brown, wooden frame. Here they sat together as a fine mist that often settled on this hill shrouded the view that should have extended to the farthest edges of the city spreading below on all sides. Here they sat, some part of her cheeks cherry red fading to a finer whiteness, uneven, as if imprinted, her hair falling in thick defined sections, straight and uncombed, sometimes across her nose, her nose with a bump and a sharp end. Fairer than her hair her eyebrows were canopies for her wide eyes. She entered the box and they sat and played in the coarse sand.

Two women sat on a green bench, their shawls blowing in the gentle breeze off the water, their hands and eyes attentive to what lay awake in the covered carriages. Pigeons settled on the various steel frames and listened to the water through the fog. From the bottom of the hill the faint squeal of trolley cars ascended as they rounded the turns and stopped, their overhead wires quivering, gleaming, and then melding into sparkling golden rods. Shrill voices kicked screen doors open, calling names and stopping as barks followed, even higher voices, then the heavy breath of running up the hill.

A driveway fell steeply, the edges of the sidewalk crumbling in big chunks of cement with granite chips embedded leading to the small grey garage where in winter they sat or leaned on the plank strung across the back, their breath steaming the windows that looked out over the park. She would reach under her jacket and lift up her skirt to wipe the fogged up windows clean. In late afternoon they walked or sat, the mist settling and hanging over the faint squeal at the bottom of the hill. Screen doors hit, swung, creaked and were latched as he slapped at garbage cans or kicked signs to make them flags in the wind on his way up the hill. Over the fence she approached, a fence he associated with her face, a particular door in a place far from this one. She pushed through the fog with a faint scent almost undetectable, her cheeks fading to a finer whiteness. Once in the light of her room as the sun came through then dimmed in the fog he sat on her bed as she changed her clothes and fixed her leg, first pouring one liquid, a clear one, then another, a red one that hurt as it ran over the wound and down the calf to her ankle after which she covered it all with a flesh-colored patch.

~

What he remembers are halls, an ominous door at the end of one, the room behind it inhabited by a boarder who seldom appeared. Stairs that weren't steep or wide led to the kitchen where a back door opened to a landing with steps of rotted wood: the third one down he avoided or would get caught and fall through, tumbling down the steps to the cement that led out to the street. Objects she placed before him at intervals, a rake, a stick, a shovel, a green ball, as an offering, her hands held out to him across the plank with her head cocked a bit to one side. He watched her, cautious, unable to say anything or return the offering through acceptance or throw the ball down the hill to watch the bark and wag of the brown dog, to be able to watch the brown dog with her. Her head remained at an angle until she became exasperated then threw the ball out the window herself as he watched water spin off the green sponge ball soaring in the empty space before it fell, outlined against the steel frame from which a blond-haired boy in a grey shirt and blue pants swung. He watched the ball hit the ground with a wet thud and bounce once or twice before it began a slow roll until the brown dog outran it, put himself in front of it and picked it up in his mouth. The dog sprawled in the weeds and stuck his right paw to his mouth turning the ball over and over as if to taste its full circumference. He watched the dog and watched her through the window as he slid down the hill to the dog. When he got to it he grabbed the ball out of the dog's mouth and threw it further, watching the ball skid, bounce and roll as she and the dog went after it.

～

Again he waited and didn't go to school. They met in the morning in back of the garage. Past the park they could see the building, huddled against the damp brick wall up to their ankles in dead leaves they watched the girls. The big old lady with the pleated skirt made the girls run before she let them play. When the old lady got to the other end of the field they saw her long blue pleats bunch against her thick legs and wide hips as they snuck out of the garage, leaned against a tree next to the fence and whistled and taunted. Sometimes one of the girls ducked behind the tree for a cigarette. As the field emptied they watched the last one's skirt bounce over bruised knees through the thick green doors with frosted glass and wire mesh in diamond pattern frozen inside. Up and down brown stairs, they'd go down brown halls and enter grey rooms. Grey rooms with shut windows, lights that flickered. Men in grey suits, women with starched dresses, black shoes, faint yellow chalk on chipped ebony boards. The rustle of clothes and hiss of radiators as the whole class stood, some voices above or below the rest, as they labored through the pledge, hands on their hearts.

When the bell rang, it echoed across the field. They kicked at the crisp leaves and walked back on the path at the edge of the park, around the side of the vacant garage, up the small hill with roots and stumps, past the yard and up to the street. A door opened and a woman stepped out of a triple-decker. She hung a green rug over the side of the porch and beat it with a mop handle she picked up from where it leaned against the edge of a windowpane that housed a sheet of cracked glass.

~

A long dark hallway led to the boiler room. On both sides of the hall doors opened into small rooms and sometimes she waited for him. He'd have to check them all and then she'd sneak around in back of him and flip the lights off in the hall and get back in one of the rooms he'd already checked. He could hear her voice and her feet as she'd go through one of the rooms with adjoining doors, flatten herself against a wall and scream as he came through. When he finally got a hold of her they'd wrestle on the cement floor. She was big, not fat, but big and strong, and she'd beat him when they wrestled, lying on top of him in the pitch black, the steam hissing from the boiler beneath her breath. She wanted a voice but all she could hear was her scream and the echo of her own footsteps past the doors. He made her follow and by the time she wondered where he'd been he jumped her from behind and they wrestled to the floor again giggling and shrieking. There was a melody she sang, one he remembered but couldn't duplicate, in a light scratchy voice as she sat opposite him at the cluttered table. The kitchen was small and stacked with shelves filled with bottles and boxes. Pots and pans hung from hooks on the greasy yellow walls. The floor glittered linoleum, tiny green, red and white squares dotted with silver over a grey base. Her room was the size of the bed with enough space to walk around it. In slow rain when he stepped from the street down the three steps to the first door then across the hall to the next it seemed as if he could squeeze it and leave a pool of water on the damp cellar floor and all that would be left of the door would be the tarnished gold handle of the bell that he held in his hand and turned.

∽

Each window was filled with the gleaming brass horns. Or they looked that way, gold and shiny, from where he was, on the sidewalk, pounding the pavement, each street leading to an alley through which he had once walked. The windows were dirty, and if the sun wasn't just right the horns didn't glow but hung there, helpless, with price tags on them.

As if it were first memory, a hall that led through

to a courtyard, shaded by small trees. Once inside there were tables of wrought iron around which older people sat, drinking from tall green, unmarked bottles. Each time he looked out the window, the view was worse, or the thought that there was a view at all that other people could see, or that if he looked there, then there would be others who could see him.

When he walked he looked at the ground or the windows. He struggled to remember the table, a big table, unpainted, unstained, simple legs, the whole thing cluttered with papers, objects. In the corners stacks leaned precariously, pens, pencils, scribbled notes, books fully open upside down with both covers visible, one on top of another surrounded by magazines, radio parts, half-used matchbooks. The table he had now was neat but his fingers picked and scratched at the damp label on the wet bottle that sat before him. Her arm swept down past her mouth as she spoke: "Five letters, they buried gasoline and shells and everything under the pyramids, each letter in Egypt stood for another stash."

He remembered the pulleys of the dumbwaiter rattling, the old woman with the tired, long white face, the eerie sheen of her thick glasses, the piercing eyes in the wooden face, the tapping of her cane against the table by the window, the click of the latch, the stream of light. Her wrinkled wrist ran back under the blanket draped across the chair, the skin stretched tight over the bridge of her nose, the polish of old ivory, the legs of the chair creaking. A door opened and someone stepped out onto the back porch of a triple-decker. She hung a green rug over the side and began beating it with a mop handle she had picked up from where it was leaning at the edge of a cracked pane of glass.

Huddled against the damp brick wall, up to their ankles in dead leaves, kids were calling under the railroad bridge. The freights came rumbling down, over a hundred cars long, the engines throwing yellow light on them as they tried to grab hold of the slow moving caravan easing into a curve or a switching track. One kid looked away from the others toward the gulls hovering over a scow filled with garbage

pulled by a barge with tires strung all around its faded crimson rails. A man in a white t-shirt tight across
the olive skin of his broad chest and big arms pulled
the string to release the whistle of the foghorn.

THE WATER

We'd ride to the bridge and I'd walk her across in my arms. We'd go home as the sun rose and get into bed and stay there till someone turned the lights back on and then we'd go back out.

There must have been some other reason.

Would it have made any difference?

You must have stopped talking.

I wanted to hold her on the boat but all we did was look at the water.

She said she waited.

She did.

We left early but all I remember were the lights over the water.

Like you'd won her off the top rack for sinking ducks or something.

What if it began with something about a car?

The first of May was grey, it rained all fucking day — how's that?

No car.

That first day of May, the right front was flat, a kid busted my window with a bat.

And we could've ridden the ferris wheel all night or dove naked into the quarries.

The field was long and flat and empty.

The woman stood out against the grey house, past boats loading and unloading, across the rocks to the end of the jetty, trawlers steaming into port.

You went north.

The roads were desolate, low fences, faded signs on rusty poles.

You had the shack that summer.

The lines on the woman's face were clean and straight. I would have gone in but I looked past her through the door and down the hall. At the end there was a window and you could see a field through it, like the house wasn't even there.

What if you just hadn't stopped?

I asked how it started.

You told me the night beckons.

⁓

He walked toward the pier and the jetty. It was cold for August and the wind swept right over the beach and onto the road, kicking up sand in its path. He walked past the gas station, waving as he did. His tired body ached all over. The bruises and cuts had begun to hurt that morning and his right leg looked as if were made of wood as he walked. He made his way past the beach and, though he was hurt, stepped nimbly up onto the rocks. He walked deliberately, picking each step slowly and carefully until he reached the end of the jetty and could walk no more. A full moon shone brightly, bringing with it the high tide, the highest of the year. Water rushed through the channel creating little whirlpools and swirls, then breakers crashing against the rocks that sprayed up to the top and over the sea wall. Fishermen were on their way in one by one, minutes or hours apart they steamed into home port, some smiling and waving and others just looking straight into the water, determined to remember how the fish got away, how the goddamn fish got away, watching the harpoon splash against the water like some sick joke, again and again. He watched the boats go by but they weren't really there, lost in the sound as he was, hypnotized by the movement of the water, bound to this ocean, watching the water move just like watching or listening to anything constant and enveloping: generators or compressors or tractors or chainsaws screaming in the woods, the constant methodical sounds of machinery, the rhythm of attention you always needed to pay the machinery. The initial shock of the accident had worn off, at least for him, and he could only consider himself lucky now sitting on the rocks, the wind blowing his jacket onto his back, watching the crazy things the water did while it rushed through the channel, the outlines of other islands barely visible across the sound. Way off in the distance across the horizon he could see what everyone called the Tower, with its red and white blinking lights faintly playing off the sound of bell buoys rolling in the dark water. It wouldn't be long now, soon he'd be back on a boat. Before closing his eyes, he lay down on a nice flat rock and watched the moon.

$\sim$

Down the road, down the road he'd skip and jump, to Josie's old man he'd go. But it started raining so he ran across the road behind the boarded-up schoolhouse to the half-buried fire engine under the wide oak tree and slid under where the pump had been until he worked his way through to the tank where it was dry. He felt something move at the other end and saw her face peek through the rungs.

"How did you know I'd be here?"

"I wanted to get out of the rain."

"I saw you by the bridge and over by the fort a couple of times."

"Why didn't you say something?"

"I couldn't."

Rain dripped off the rungs and settled in puddles by his feet. "Come on up here, it's dry." He got a foothold and grabbed for a rung, swinging his hips so his feet flew forward and hooked in. He worked his way down the ladder with his back to the ground that way before swinging up and through feet first, hips doubled, knees and back bent till at last his head popped through and his eyes caught the dense green.

"Not bad, not bad at all. And you've never shimmied a mast? Or tight-roped a flying bridge?" He looked up, over, around, and to the back of him.

"You want to come over?"

"I was on my way."

~

He hadn't thought of her or the place he'd lived then for a long time. He had spent a lot of time with her and her family. He lived across the road, down the hill by the pond. The house he lived in was small, a shack. The door opened to a kitchen he had to crouch in over the oven or the sink, the ceiling was so low. Light could be seen through cracks almost the whole length of it, and mice had chewed a small hole under the sink. He left a can in front of the hole. When he heard them scratch in the middle of the night he got up and took the gun he kept against the refrigerator, kicked the can away, and shot at them.

It was difficult to hit a mouse in a hole in the dark but he got pretty good at it. A cat began to come and feed on the remains that lay scattered by the gas tanks. A girl down the road took the cat and let it stay at her house. He saw it a few times walking the length of her small porch when the sun was out. She fed it regularly. It got fat and lazy and no longer cared about mice. The remains stayed longer then but soon other animals came. Some of them fought and he'd hear them scurry under the house. Once he got up to shoot but the flashlight strapped to his gun lit up a skunk so he let it go.

∽

His intentions had been clear once, he wanted to say, though he knew she'd be standing in a cutting shed shucking scallops soon enough. The days would get shorter and the wind would have more bite to it but there would always be wood in a stack in the corner of the shed to put in the stove. They'd been together those few hours, stumbling along the Midway in the summer air, tossing nickels and rings, pitching balls, throwing at baskets, and sinking ducks as they held each other up. Someone had come back from town with another bottle and they all walked in through the field by the horse track and sat in the grass watching the ferris wheel and listening to the carnies hawk their wares: "Only once around the ring, bring your baby back a teddy bear. Once, twice, try it again, only once around the ring makes you a winner." Or: "This one's a game of skill, just one lucky lever, let's go, who's got the lucky lever, just one lucky lever," as a rubber ball bounced from a scoop triggered by a rod and fell through a hole that pushed a spring and sent a little metal horse forward, twelve little metal horses down the line, only one winner, no place or show. It had been years since he'd worked the breakdown, using the heavy ratchets

and breaker bars to unbolt the framework of the ferris wheel or crawling in the mud under the Whirling
Dervish or the Stinger to loosen the hinges. Late at
night, his feet aching and back sore, he'd leave the
fairgrounds alone with the sun almost up and walk
the long road back to the sea, just to jump in and
cool off. He got tired of it, though, and got a job at
the gas station.

They would have rested easily in each other's
arms, laying a little drunk in the grass as things
were shutting down, had it not been for the bright
lights and sharp crackle of a voice through a bull-
horn. Apparently, someone had stolen the cruiser
and decided to drive it right through the grounds.
Before they knew it, all hell broke loose. Caldwell
— having jumped off a trailer to commandeer the
cruiser and bring it to a stop after it careened off a
fence and slid halfway across the track — was tap-
dancing on the hood, his shirt ripped in more than
a few places and his pants hanging down almost past
his hips. Lights came on as the carnies peered out
of their trailers, all lined in rows, rippled aluminum

and straight stainless, lime-green, white, pink, blue and red, some with little flowerboxes hanging out the windows.

"Raul stole a sack full of corn," he drawled, "he was in the truck with Sally, you shoulda seen him. We let 'em have it, smearing corn all over the windows, her neck, his back." He gritted his teeth and shook his head in jerks. "Somebody get me home."

Someone pulled a spyglass out of the back of their truck, got down on one knee to spot the prey and started yelling: "Breacher, breacher, man the harpoons."

"All the meat you can eat, none too fresh, I'm afraid." Someone else propped Caldwell against a pile of boxes and took a hat to put over his face.

"What a mess," Casey said, his ear to Caldwell's stomach.

"Do I get him by the pound or by the mile?" asked the voice from the cab of the pick-up, as it pulled up to hoist him aboard.

"Just get him home."

"I always knew he was a jerk," said Borneo,

"the old man'll come and blame it on me, it's always me."

The fingers on Casey's left hand picked at the air, the fingers on his right strumming. He began to sing:

> I never went on safari
> Unless I went with my Mata Hari
> Cause I left my blunderbussy

Gordon came in on "blunderbussy" and a few others, holding each other up, came in too:

> So far, so far far away, so far away
> From Borneo
> Oh no,
> I won't go on no safari

Bet and Allie came in:

> Without my only Mata Hari

Casey got down on one knee at Borneo's feet, his right arm extending to his chest. Allie undid one button of her shirt and pulled it down her shoulder, fluttering her eyelids: "O Borneo, wherefore art thou Borneo?"

"Knight me, sire, knight me," Casey said, his head bowed to the ground. Borneo turned, looking down at his subject. "And pray tell, my daughter, my good daughter, with Morgan's son," Casey's huge arm smothering Josie. "Captain Morgan. Protector of the sea."

"King of tin!"

"Keep it up, kid."

"I'm going blind," said Borneo.

"Oh, no," they answered.

"Who threw out my keys and trampled my wife's garden?"

"The king of tin," all answered, "the king of tin!"

～

When he went to sign the "insurance" policy, the table of losses had a desperate hilarity to it: one eye: fifteen-hundred; two fingers: one thousand; one hand: thirty-five hundred; toes: two-fifty apiece; loss of leg or legs, and so on, continuing for two pages with all possible combinations. There'd been a few close calls, and he'd been witness to hands caught in winches, dropped trailers, exploding acetylene tanks, and a variety of other things that hadn't led to anyone's death but conformed to the chart of losses, excluding burns and skin grafts.

He first met Caldwell at the boat. He saw someone he recognized step out of the passenger side of the cab of a Mack, Nap's friend, who'd driven to the hospital with them after the accident. They greeted each other and Sam asked him where they were heading. Eric pointed to the leaky trailer and said: "Fish." He pulled some papers out of the top pocket of a green-and-black mackinaw and pointed toward the freight office. Sam made out the lights of the ferry in the fog and watched it come through the mist so thick the spotlights on the frame of the slip couldn't cut through it. Another man walked out of the freight office with Eric and they stopped for a minute before turning back. The man walked up to Sam's car and stopped to admire it: "Forty-one?"

Sam nodded. The man stuck his head through the driver's side window. "Island car?"

"Nope, from up north."

The man smiled. "I used to have a lot of these. No room, though, with those," and he pointed to the green Mack on whose fifth wheel a diesel-blackened trailer rested with the huge yellow word COLLOSAL painted on the side. A man on the ferry set the winch, tightened the cables, and dropped the chain as cars began driving off over the steel plate lid, making it bang before their tires grabbed asphalt and drove away. After they got on deck, they went to the lunch counter, Caldwell having a beer and Eric and Sam talking about Nap. At some point Caldwell asked Sam where he was going and said that maybe it didn't make much sense to go anywhere but that he should stay around or come back and, as he put it, "join the organization," in which, as he also put it, "we might just have a spot." When Eric saw the lights of the mainland he said they should go down to pull the plugs and dump the buckets. Sam followed them to the truck and watched as they circled the trailer and pulled cork plugs from under it to let the melting ice and fish slime pour through to the buckets they'd set underneath. Then they dumped the buckets out the porthole and Eric got a jerry can out of the cab and poured its contents around the spots they'd drained, the sharp smell of chlorine filling the air. Later he'd learn this was all an elaborate method of getting rid of as much of the fish smell as possible since on the return they'd haul furniture, something the "organization" didn't usually have a permit for. Manny Ferrera edged by them, clapping his hands and shouting "clean up, Pat, come on Patty," he chided, "clean it all up," chuckling his way through the line of cars and trucks till he ducked under a chain that stretched the width of the stern and hung off two posts. He went to the wheel and started spinning it with a ratchet before continuing by hand. A few of the other men ducked under the chain to give him a hand. They brought both doors all the way back and the lights of the mainland remained shrouded in mist until they were almost in the slip. The ferry bounced off the pilings and creaked before it came to rest, the water churning white as car doors opened and engines fired while the men hooked the cables to eye-loops on shore, first cranking it fast then slower as the cable got tighter and the ferry settled and was fully docked. Sam hung off the Mack with one arm on the mirror post, the other gripping a handle, one foot on the step and the other on one of the gas tanks as Caldwell fired it up, jumping off only to watch the trailer block the entire opening of the ferry as it snaked its way out to land.

∽

The rain slowly turned to sleet and before they were out of town it had become light snow. By the time they got on the turnpike and emerged from the tunnel the city was bathed in it. The further north the bigger, wider, and thicker the flakes got. By the time they'd passed the suburbs and gotten to that long stretch of hills that followed, the fifth of Canadian Club he'd bought at the state store and ran across the highway with was finished. At the border of the next state Delfarno appeared by their side. Delfarno carried steel and his trailer had a sag in the middle of it from the extra weight. He always ran overweight at night and the worse the weather the better for him. They kept close on the flats but up-hill Delfarno fell behind as Caldwell put the pedal to the floor, lashing the dashboard with one hand as he commanded his horses to go all out. Downhill all that could be seen of Delfarno were his taillights, two of which were out, as they followed the sway of his trailer from side to side sliding along the slick road. As they passed him again on the way up a hill, Sam could make out through the snow and ice on the windshield the words on the back of his trailer: WHERE'D HE GO, THAT CRAZY DELFARNO! in neat silver cursive with a black border that was chipped along the edges of the lettering.

～

The white paint peeled off the old dilapidated building in chunks and rolls. The weeds grew up to and over the loading dock. A few old delivery trucks hugged the back wall and weeds grew through the seats, the hoods, and out the windows. Every now and then someone walked out of one of the walk-in freezers, across the loading dock and into the tiny cubicle that served as the office. Wind rolled gently off the harbor, past the brightly painted boats that bobbed in the deep blue water, green and red with white numbers painted on the sides and nets hanging from the sterns. Cars drove by occasionally, the sun glistening off their tops and hoods.

Caldwell maneuvered the Freightliner around the corner and pulled the trailer up several hundred yards past the building. Sam jumped out of the rig and directed him into the slot in front of the loading dock. Caldwell let the motor run for a few minutes before he shut it off. Smoke belched out of the twin pipes, making a small black cloud that floated away in the blue sky. Caldwell got out of the truck holding some papers. They walked across the loading dock and into the office.

Behind the single grey desk sat a woman of about fifty. She wore blue slacks and a white cotton shirt. Behind her on the wall were calendars with various pictures of butter, cottage cheese, buttermilk, ice cream, cream cheese, and milk. The desk was covered with papers and envelopes. She rummaged around in them and gave one to Caldwell in exchange for his.

They went back outside. Caldwell pulled the pin on the trailer and Sam went around to the side to let the dolly wheels down. They each unhooked an air hose and snapped them into their holders in back of the cab. Caldwell let Sam drive the cab back to where the other trailers were parked on a strip of land that lay between a small road lined with pink and green houses and a stand of power lines. Many of the houses had a junked car in the back and a coop out front with chickens or pigs. Sam backed the cab up to the trailer, lined it up, then slammed it in till the pin locked. Seven smashed cars sat on the trailer — a '62 Galaxy, '58 Star-Fire, '60 Falcon, '59 Mercury, '63 Comet, '64 Dynamic-88, and a '51 Olds Rocket. Cars people had been killed in or got disgusted with, their rods knocked, their valves tapped, engines seized. Stripped of all their useful parts they sat in weeds where kids played in them, animals lived in them, or the junk man put a few dollars down to haul them away.

He couldn't remember if they had thrown pebbles or sand at each other. He saw her legs for a second, then again as they appeared under a chassis or though a door. He had been playing with her on the swings across the street from the garage, the swing she flew off as she ran across the field, telling him she'd beat him to the junkyard. He chased her over, past the white fence, across the street, past the gas pumps and the air hose, through the mud by the tin shacks whose doors rattled and swung in the wind, all the way to the yard filled with ancient, smashed cars. She ran through them, opening doors, jumping across hoods and roofs, taunting him with sand or pebbles. Glass crunched and doors rattled as he landed running, the sand hitting hollow fenders and crumbling back to the ground. Past a tall fence the field opened up to a lush green where the brook turned into a river. She jumped the fence and he chased her through the tall grass, up a dirt road, through some woods and someone's yard where she fell onto her back in the moist, thick growth and laughed at the sky. He stood at a distance and watched her until she sat up and looked at him. He walked over and sat next to her. They stayed there, watching each other and an old man stepping out of a shack to feed his chickens across the river.

～

As drunk as they were now the water chilled them to the bone. The waves broke at random, some breaking farther out than others. A strong undertow knocked them off their feet. Sarah's hair was deep black against the red cliffs and hung over her shoulders and across her breasts. Sam swam straight out beyond the breakers. He stopped and floated on his back. She stayed closer to shore and dove under the waves before they broke. They got out of the water and he chased her across the beach to the wall of cliffs where they both collapsed in the sand. They lay there against the cliffs, leaning on each other.

Cold is what he wanted to say to her. The house would be cold soon.

Fix it, she would tell him.

Wind swept off the sound, the cliffs turned grey as the sun dipped under the water. They put their clothes on and walked.

He pulled the car up to the house. She got out first and went in. He heard the door, then another one. He got out slowly, put the keys on the visor, and shook the sand out of his pants. He closed the car door and stood in the yard looking at the tiny house. He went in and stood in the kitchen. Light could be seen through the ceiling from one end to the other. When the wind came up it swept through the house and rattled the window-frames. He kept standing there, just looking out the window at the car in the empty field.

~

A bitter wind blew off the pond the day Eric and Nap gunned for ducks. In the flats they knelt behind the tall grass and watched the tips stretched back taut by the breeze and kept there until the point it seemed they would break. Nap used his call to bring out the ducks. They missed some that flew far, skidded on the water and flew off again as their shots scattered, making rings in the water around them. They walked up the hill, through the marshes and over Benton's fence, around the bend to the inlet. Six ducks flew over the rocks, Eric got the top one, leading it right and dropping it. Then he heard "goddamn," and, "it's jammed" as he turned to hear a shot that shouldn't have gone off and saw the gun dance on its own in the air before falling through the tall grass to the hard ground.

Nap held the hand in front of his face, the skin peeled back from the hole the shot had blown in his palm. The blood ran down his wrist and soaked the sleeve of his army jacket, turning it brown. Galdraf was barking and scampering through the grass to retrieve the lead duck. Eric grabbed Nap by the waist and with his other arm picked up the gun that lay on the ground.

"Where's my glove?" said Nap, sharp, his eyes

wide open and staring straight ahead, the hand still held in the air, skin apart from bone, the inner works showing.

"Later, I'll get your fucking glove later."

Nap walked ahead, almost marching, tripping on branches and bumping into rocks. Eric let him wander ahead as he stopped and slit a piece of his sleeve off with his knife. He dropped both guns by a bush he knew he'd remember and ran ahead.

"Stop," he said, then shouted, "STOP!" pulling Nap up short by the collar of his coat as he told him to hold it. He took the strip of cloth and tied it around Nap's wrist. Pulling it tight, he put a knot on it with a trailer that he held on to so the hand remained upright. They got to the path through the woods and over the brook that led to the road.

"What about my glove?"

"Fuck the glove, I'll get it, forget it, don't worry, I'll get your goddamn glove."

"You should've bought the whole box, number fours, it's cheaper that way."

"Jesus Christ."

At the end of the clearing was a house and the noise of men working on it. Eric broke from Nap and ran. He tore the screen door open to see a ladder with someone on it nailing a piece of wood to the ceiling.

"I got to use the phone!" Another face appeared from the back room, an arm holding a saw.

"Get a towel," Eric shouted as he dialed.

The one on the ladder came down quickly and went to a room where he got a towel out of a chest of drawers. He tossed it to the other guy who had put down the saw and caught it as it flapped through the doorway. Eric was off the phone, had grabbed the towel and was out the door.

Nap stood in the middle of the field and yelled "Galdraf! Galdraf!" over and over, "Galdraf!" as he turned slowly in a circle he had formed for himself, "Draffy!" turning slightly and calling, "Draffy!" turning and calling, again and again, his whole sleeve brown by now. Eric wrapped the towel around the hand.

"He's got the duck, you got the lead one."

"He'll get it, he'll get it," Eric said.

Abe looked at Nap's hand and turned. Eric looked at the car in front of the house then out the road and up the hill. Abe came back with a bottle of whiskey that he held up for Nap.

"The gun jammed."

They nodded.

"Where is that bastard," he looked at the road and paced out toward it a few steps, then back.

Nap called for Galdraf again and told Eric his old man would be mad if he didn't find the glove.

Sam and Abe stood and looked up the hill at the road.

"That no good bastard," Eric paced back and forth.

"Fuck it, let's go."

"I'll take him down," said Sam, and he told Abe to wait. They got in the black sedan, Nap lay across the back with his hand draped across where the front seats folded, Eric holding the whiskey bottle and Sam honking and keeping the lights on as they sped off the dirt and out onto the main road.

～

Casey pulled his head out from under the hood and took his eyes off the engine he'd been working on. He brushed his forearm against his forehead and looked out to the sun that bleached the field. The horse was still and had its head under the slight shade the shed made. Every now and then his tail went around in a slow lazy arc. No wind, no birds. A few flies buzzed in and out of the shade of the garage and the paint on some of the cars littered along the hill glimmered. The scratches on the windshields showed, circles and circles of them covered with dirt and bird-shit. The pigs had no shade to go under so they just sat still, sweating.

Before he got up over the hill Sam heard wrenches drop as Casey rummaged through his box and muttered as he tossed sockets and box ends out from under each other. By the time Sam got to him his head was back under and his huge shoulders and back covered most of the motor. Legs in the air, he balanced his stomach on the grill and fan shroud, his right elbow coming up and down as he worked at a nut. Sam peeked in at the other side. The wrench caught, Casey's elbow jogged, and it slipped off the nut.

Casey garbled something and leaned further in, his feet up higher than his back. Sam turned and knelt to the green shell box that sat on the dirty floor. He waved a fly off the sockets. He gave Casey a wrench, picked the one up that Casey had let drop, and tossed it back into the shell box. He walked to the edge of the shade and looked out to the field. Josie and her little brother came up past the road and waved as they went in the house. Her mother came out the other door and put a shirt on the line. Casey came from the back of the garage with two bottles. Sam uncapped his and took a long drink. Casey went over and sat on a pile of blocks stacked near the door.

"Two weeks", he said.

Sam nodded. Casey shook his head and downed the rest of the beer. He went to the cooler and came back with another one.

"He's alright I guess."

"I wish she was mine. I wish she left. I wish she was somebody else's."

"What'll you do, leave?" Sam heard a screen door snap back against its frame and looked up to the house to see Billy walk around to the other side of it.

Casey looked in the other direction. A bird called and its wings fluttered against the leaves. It took off and went to rest on top of the pilothouse of a trawler nestled between an oak and a pile of rusted trucks.

"Yesterday was the first time I'd ever talked to Josie about him since the funeral."

"You want a goddamn medal?"

"It's been five years, Casey, for chrissake."

Casey winged the bottle against the hull of the trawler. The bird started and flew to a tree. Sam went to the cooler for more beer. Casey snapped the catch down on the shell box and kicked it against the wall in the corner. He pulled down on the hood of the car and slammed it shut.

"Let's take a ride."

They walked out of the garage around to the back of it and got in the green Jeep. Casey pulled out of the dirt around to the front. Sam got out and put air in one of the front tires. He took the rest of the beer out of the cooler and put it in the front seat. As he stepped in, Casey spun out of the sand in front of the garage and drove across the field toward the back road.

~

I'll stay, as they say here, the winter. Abe came for a few weeks and helped with the house. We finished the insulation then dug a trench and sunk the pipes. I met a guy named Caldwell and went to work for him. He's got a trucking company, even incorporated. He's got this driveway and he's got this basement he uses as an office and he's got all these trucks and he never sleeps and his trucks are anywhere from Maine to Florida. Along with all that and his wife and kids and his ex-wife and other kids and mortgages and banknotes and loan sharks, he's got me. I collect bills, answer the phone, go to banks, drive trucks, load and unload, take care of the kids, bullshit people for him, and anything else you can think of. Casey lives over the hill. Casey that I've told you about. I spend more time there than I should. Me and his daughter get drunk a lot. He thinks he's my father. Or else he wants me to be his son. He wants me to be his son that got killed. His other daughter just got married. She turned seventeen right after the wedding. Casey has the bug too. He wants to get married but he already is. So he screams at his wife and shows up once every few weeks to feed the horses or throw wrenches around the garage. I spend a lot of time sleeping in trucks. Waiting for guys to open the doors after they've combed their hair and polished their forklifts. What can I say? I think of us on subways, always on a subway on our way to no place special. Over the hill there's Casey. And his daughter. And his other daughter. And his little son who walks over the hill and knocks on my window to wake me up Sunday mornings to shoot at cans down by the pond. He waits outside. I grumble but I always get dressed and go get the gun. We run down the dirt road together. Over the fence to the banks of the pond kicking at stones and hoping an arrowhead shows.

Little Billy's got the gun. Casey's dead. No one ever lived in that house. His horses jumped the fence. Years they've wandered. Empty fields. His sister's gone. A stone's supposed to be his brother.

Out on the water Billy watches a bird. He pulls the trigger. The wings flap. The bird drops still and floats. We walk more, look for ducks, shoot at cans. After a while I tell him it's late and we walk back to the house. I tell him they'll miss him, to go home.

SNAPSHOT

"That's what he said he wanted"

"Couldn't have done it."

"The goddamn thing was split right down the rail, ran the length of it."

"Looking scared boy, I ain't seen you in Sunday clothes since you were a little shit."

"He had a Detroit but the fucking thing blew oil like crazy. Then the winter without the pan after he'd hauled it out and it lay in the shed like that, bearings froze and two rods snapped — it cracked on number four, right through the goddamn sleeve."

"Call him whatever you want but he's a real son of a bitch."

"Who said that?"

"Elbows and assholes. Goddamnit, that's all they say, elbows and assholes — they just turned and stuck their heads underwater, you should have seen it!"

"Right over the bulkhead, and when they saw the lights, just elbows and assholes. Fell flat he did right over the fucking edge. I saw him that time, there was nothing else anyone could do. He just let go right over the side like that . . ."

"Where the hell did he go?"

"That sonofabitch couldn't find the goddamn zipper if he had to piss and I mean quick — let the little shit drown for all I care, it's good for the boy."

"Sam, get over there with Josie, behind, like that. Where the hell is Billy? Move the flowers, get that crap out of the way."

"Put your arm around her, there, right by that swordfish."

"Get that fucking thing away from my ear!"

"Ready?"

∽

Sam pulled the car into the pebble filled lot, his headlights flashed past the rear door and he saw them in there, the steam rising as they fidgeted and adjusted their tight white uniforms between armloads of dishes. He parked, shut the car off and sat finishing a cigarette before he got out and lazily walked to the door. He nodded hellos in general and a few in particular and leaned against an unused sink watching the doors swing open and closed as water hit the hot pans, bursting into a quick crescendo before getting wiped down and put back into action. The dishwasher leaned over the sink with his gaze pointed at a spot of stainless steel between the faucets as he caressed the dishes. Every now and then he stopped to take a deep breath and stare at the spot where the ceiling met the wall.

Sam got a cup of chowder and some crackers that he dropped into the thick, steaming liquid. Sarah sped by with an armload of dishes and dropped them into the sink. She walked by Sam and brushed her hand across his shoulder and told him to wait a minute. He said he wasn't going anywhere and left his hand around the slope of her hip as the cook loaded her tray with steaming plates of broiled fish and lobsters with potatoes wrapped in shiny tinfoil on the side.

He wondered about how he had thought of her, when she galloped by the house that day on a brown horse, peeking through the curtain of his room as he watched her straddling the beast as it bounced along. He walked out of the room and through the woods to stop at the clearing by the path, knowing she would pass. Her name was carved into a large tree rooted to the center of the clearing whose needles made a more than comfortable bed of the hard earth. Along with hers were other names he knew and some he had heard etched skillfully and laboriously into the thick crusty bark of the big pine. She guided the horse to a graceful stop in front of him as he sat with his back against the tree. She stayed on the horse and he stood up brushing needles from his clothes. She gave him her hand and he pulled himself up behind her. She let the horse walk to the path where she made him begin a canter that quickly turned into a gallop. He remembered her laughter and how tightly he gripped her waist.

∼

In August the air remained still and untouched, even here as close to the water as they were. Casey had been left at the bar at the point of becoming maudlin. Not wanting to knuckle under to the liquor, Sam had left as the vague uneasiness had turned to a gnawing want, no matter that the air outside was even warmer, only that it was air, and a change.

He had stood with Casey where the bar curved, making an almost perfect J. Casey leaned on the bar with one arm across Sam's shoulder.

"Then I'll have to smile and shake all their hands. Caldwell knows, those bastards, he'll tell you, she'll have to live in that lousy shack, then they'll turn around and keep trying to kick my ass out of town."

His arm got heavier and heavier on Sam's shoulder as his words ran closer and closer together, and the phone at the bar rang again, and for the third time Arthur told Casey it was his old lady and was he here yet and for the third time he wasn't, and then Casey's girl walked through the door and Sam slapped Casey on the back, swallowed the last of the beer and said he'd stop at the house tomorrow.

He found himself, though he knew it was late, after driving as if asleep on roads he knew every bend of with the radio playing and all the windows of the hardtop rolled down with air rushing through and over and across him, at the parking lot, and before he knew it, against the sink in the steaming kitchen sipping hot chowder with Sarah next to him.

He got some hot bread, an ear of corn, and a few bottles of cold beer. He took these and walked to the bulkhead where he sat watching the water toss an oversize orange raft that was attached to shore with a bright yellow cord tied around a steel shaft bolted to the bulkhead. Here he sat for some time finishing the first beer slowly then sipping steadily on the next. He walked to the gas station and looked through the window at the shiny globe nailed to the far wall beneath the rod rack and the sunglasses display and saw that it was time to go back.

~

Shielding his eyes from the high beams of a departing truck, Sam pulled into the pebbly lot. As the truck drove off behind him, Sarah reached her hand out and he pulled her from the cement step she had been sitting on. A few people milled about at the front door of the place, the older ones giving directions to the younger ones, cars stopping with doors opening and people making their way in and out. Dave pulled in with the garbage truck, his worn army jacket a constant reminder of where he'd been. They waved at him, Sarah's white uniform smooth in Sam's hand as she leaned across the front seat, her head on his shoulder as they pulled out of the lot and started driving.

Once they got to her place, he slumped across the couch and turned the radio on. It was an old model with a stained finish on its wooden case and white plastic buttons that ran across the front along the bottom. He ran the dial around the horn once to make sure it worked then brought it back to the station it had been on. Sarah came out of her room and into the living room wearing an old blue work shirt that almost reached her knees. She pushed Sam over on the couch and lay down next to him. It wasn't just her he embraced but what he could see from the corner of his eye, the bland bleached paneling that adorned the walls, the thick green carpets that covered the wood beneath them, a faint smell of newness that pervaded the chairs and the couch. Being there forced him to recall her exact scent and the weight of his grip on her waist as they galloped across the field on her brown horse, or the touch of the shingles against the small of his back as they lay on the roof in the breeze and looked across Eyeglass Pond. As they galloped across the shingles in their bare feet a dish broke and a door opened and unsure steps worked their way around furniture followed by a long inarticulate slur. Sarah's mother pushed her way past a chair and stumbled to the couch where they had already sat up at attention, side by side.

He couldn't make out everything she said as she

leaned over the radio with her arm on Sam's shoulder and spoke toward his face with a closeness she couldn't afford her daughter. Sarah pushed her over so she landed on the couch in a heap. They started arguing and Sarah's voice rose above her mother's mumbling as it broke into sobs and silence.

Beside them in those rooms that provided more space than either of them needed Sam had an overwhelming urge to tell Sarah that she knew who her father was but he got up and just left them there together on the couch. Straightening his clothes, he walked through the kitchen and out the screen door into the now cool night.

⁓

Sam and Abe stumbled up the rocky dirt road to the top of the hill and across the path in the field onto the main road. Once around the curve the sun came out. They hopped the split-rail fence to Casey's house and Sam, second to go over, stumbled on a root and fell into some bushes. The sun came directly over the hill past Liz Scott's and bleached the freshly painted clapboards of Casey's wall. The field between Scott's and Casey's looked burnt from the sun. The old lady's cats walked through the stubble of weeds and grass, slow and lazy. She took the ticks off and kept them pickled in jars all around the house.

They stood before the wall and Abe called Josie. A head stuck out they could barely see save the strands of black hair that blew through the window and stood out against the wall. They looked harder and with their hands over their eyebrows to shield the whiteness of the wall they saw a towel that went across the top of Josie's breasts and her hands that held it there.

"You don't want to be late Josie."

She looked out at them, secured the towel around her shoulders and stuck her head out a little further.

"Come on, we'll be late," Sam said.

"They already left."

Sam and Abe looked at each other.

"You're supposed to come with us."

"Late for what?"

They started to laugh and Abe handed the bottle

he had uncapped back to Sam. He took a long draw, capped it, and gave it back to Abe.

"Maybe to the jetty."

"Come on, Josie, we're late."

"Let us in, Josie, let us in, come on, let your hair down, Josie."

They had looked so long the wall stood out starkly. All behind was black, with tiny yellow spots from the sun they saw when they blinked. She started to laugh too and turned around. She let the towel drop. They saw the sun on her smooth back, then her arms went up as she slipped a shirt over her head.

They walked to the porch. On the other side of the house the whole hill was filled with Casey's junk. Cars were piled in the bushes — tractors, trailers, rotten wood, old boats and cables, ratchets and cranks and motors. The boom from his old power-wagon stuck up past the trees and the old blue paint had a faint glimmer to it. Past the junk was the other house, the one Min had put together from driftwood, hulls, cabins and planks from trawlers.

Relish was flat out in the dirt. His thick black tail

made motions against the flies. Every now and then he let his lips open, gritted his teeth and brought his huge head back. He got up, ambled toward the fence and stuck his head in a chipped bathtub. His head came out with his tongue hanging and he dipped it into a gas tank Casey had torched in half to keep the oats in. A bale of hay lay next to a little shed.

"Ever been there?" Sam said as he looked past the cats in the field to Liz Scott's.

"Once."

They laughed.

Sam picked a piece of a motor up and tossed it toward some bushes in front of the pigpen. It cut through the bushes and the pigs jumped and squealed and ran around in circles. A truck went by on the main road, and they watched the trail of black smoke drift and fade. From past Eyeglass Pond came the din of squawks as the geese circled and headed out on their evening jaunt. Abe picked up the noise and saw the lead one as he soared past the trees near the white steeple of the church. The rest followed in a perfect V.

A few shots echoed.

The screen door opened and Josie looked out to the geese.

"Probably the old man," she said.

"Wouldn't be like him to shoot in season," said Sam.

Josie sat between them.

Abe offered her the bottle. She uncapped it, had a few sips and gave it to Sam.

"I guess they'll get married," she said.

"I was in the bar yesterday, we already went through it."

"He scares me, Sam."

Abe looked out at the field of cats — they slowly walked toward the old lady's.

"He came home the other night, he hadn't been home in a week. I was in my room and I watched Billy, he just sat on his knees behind the woodstove and watched. He had my mother on the couch and he threw her around before he fell over on the table and passed out."

Abe shook his head.

"He wants the house, I guess, he wants to move in with that —" she spat a name and reached for the bottle.

"Billy walked over the hill the other day. I let him use my .22 and we walked down to the pond and shot cans."

"He's got to get out of here, it's worst for him."

They were silent. Another truck went by on the main road. The field had worked its way to orange and the leaves on the trees whispered in a light breeze that came off the pond. Abe took another sip. The bottle went back down the line: Josie had some, then gave it to Sam.

"I'll never forget that day he picked me up. I got in and he was yelling but he wasn't really yelling, it was just loud, that goddamn voice that goes through you, about the goddamn roads and goddamn traffic and goddamn this and goddamn that and lousy goddamn tires and kids that drove too goddamn fast and he went right through the stop sign at the corners. I got out at the top of the hill as he turned in. An hour later Billy called and told me Lee got killed."

Josie's head hung and dropped into Sam's lap. He felt something wet and her hands tremble as they held his leg. He ran his hand through her hair.

"Now look what you did," said Abe. "Josie, come on Josie, let's go get drunk Josie."

Josie lifted her head up and Sam wiped the tears off her cheeks with the sleeve of his shirt.

Abe picked the bottle up. They got off the porch and walked over the hill toward the pond.

BLUE-GREY

Eric longed for a day when the wind blew, when it would beat against his face until his cheeks stung, till he could no longer feel the toes at the ends of his feet. Winter here was an on and off thing, and the ponds seldom froze to a degree that allowed them to be walked or skated on. As Mr. Hafferty had said, the wind was balmy, and he'd repeated it a few times for lack of anything better. In the little sun there was when it broke through the dense bulk of grey to pierce the fog, Mr. Hafferty stood with his paper against the doorway between the drugstore and Red Man's Hall. Eric looked through the space between the two buildings and past the cement stairs out to sea.

Mr. Hafferty said the main thing was to get away from the familiar spots that he now could only see without her. Eric had a sense of that but wanted it left alone, for himself. Everyone has to die, he wanted to say, but knew that wouldn't do, faced with it, when it came to that.

"When I was in the library this morning they asked about her, the older woman with the glasses, she had been on vacation and hadn't heard," Mr. Hafferty laughed a bit, his hat pushed back. He looked where Eric gazed.

"Some boys always wanted to go to sea. Somehow it never appealed to me. I guess there was never much time to consider it."

The young man turned, leaning his elbows on the rail. A bit of orange juice worked its way up his throat, rested on his tongue. He spit toward the water.

"There was some research they had done, I was called in, mentioned in one of the studies, I'll show it to you sometime, quite interesting."

They were silent and Mr. Hafferty looked to the paper for something to talk about.

"I understand they're going ahead with tearing down Brown's."

"There was a row about the whole thing." He adjusted his glasses at the end of his nose and propped the paper up against the wind as Eric glanced over his shoulder.

"We used to fish on the rocks by Brown's."

They greeted Armstrong as he straight-armed the door of the drugstore on his way out.

"That's when my old man had the place on the other side, by the cut."

"Oh," said Mr. Hafferty, his white eyebrows rising. "Another thing I never really did." He looked at his feet and the ground around them.

"Then the Moors burned and we kids got chased wherever we went."

"Remember once that whale washed up, wasn't that big I recall, as far as whales go anyway. That was the thing to see. Emily and I walked from our place, it was on the beach over at the turn by the wharves."

"Where the swings were, across from Bunker's Marine, I was about seven."

"Awful the way they finally shoveled the thing onto dump trucks after they'd sawed it up."

"East Main stunk worse than it does anyway."

"Remember Lorna? Worked over at the fountain?"

"Sure."

Mr. Hafferty smiled, trying to refold the paper. Wind cut the half-sheets in quarters, the sections clung to each other.

"That's when you have to hold on. I'm just not sure. A friend of my brother's invited me up north for a visit. Should be nice up there this time of year. Me and Madden are going up next week. You met Madden some time ago, that night at the Rose, I think. There was a question of some romantic attachment I had with the man's sister, she remembered I'd been around the house a lot those days. All I said was look on me as a brother, that I wasn't old enough to be looked at as a father. My son Paul got a kick out of it."

The fog had begun to lift. Slowly the sun fought its way through the thickness that enveloped them. A few trawlers could be seen in the distance.

"Hello."

Eric turned slightly to see Woolner walk toward Manner's.

"Woolner," Eric nodded. Mr. Hafferty faced the street. He looked down the end of it toward the fork where the library was. The young man continued with the sea. Feeling more gas from the juice, he lit a cigarette.

"A man asked me, quite some time ago, about a study that had been done, a lord, some letters to his son. I had quite a bit of the material, he's from one of the universities, I guess he'll come up."

"What happened to Lorna?"

"She married this guy, you probably don't —" Mr. Hafferty shrugged that off and stopped a second. "Out at the end of Slip Road where the Tides is now there used to be a, you know where the little horse riding place is?"

Eric smiled. Mr. Hafferty continued.

"Behind down Simpson Road was where they had a small base, something to do with the Air Force. The guy worked on the planning end of it. See, she'd

gone out with Paul for the longest time then suddenly they just stopped, we never talked about it. Of
course Paul was gone by then but we still saw Lorna,
and his name was Ed. They're in the Midwest now,
that's where he was from."

"I almost broke my neck on those two-bit nags
they had. I think they got the damn things wild and
doped them up or something but every now and
then they really threw."

"Paul was a lifeguard at Good Harbor the summer before he left."

"My brother almost drowned there, further
down by the bridge. We used to walk out to Rock
Island at low tide. That time a rip caught him, sucked
him under. I just dove off the bridge when I saw him
kick. An older guy, strong swimmer, grabbed his leg,
pulled him over his shoulder and rode him in."

"I never swam much. Sometimes in the lake or
when the quarries were low. The waves were too
rough for me."

~

Sun shone in spots on the trawlers. Eric had left Hannah Morrison and walked into the rain without hat or coat. They'd walked past Russet's, the Gansett, the Wesley, around Elk's Nook to Ruby's. One light put the porch in focus, and Ruby, alone in the front room behind the screen door. She hummed with her eyes closed, her neck easy against the back of her rocker.

"Keep those closed, lady."

She continued the hum then broke with a grin. "It's late boy, you been gone too long."

"Only watching the water, Ruby."

"Who's with you?"

"You know."

Ruby tilted her head back, reached deep and got in "Take 9, on the hook by the door," before the resonance of her laughter resounded, filling the air. Ruby heard Eric's steps and the key against the hook as he removed it. She listened to those steps and the extra set that followed as they scurried up the stairs. She remained in her chair with her head tilted back, continuing to hum with her eyes closed.

The light that woke them was grey and crept through the room they lay in. Hannah reached her hand to his forehead and let it rest there, her fingers running through the hair near his ear. Smoke from her cigarette curled and hung above them, the room damp, with their eyes open they knew the room was damp, and through the delicate old curtains Ruby had picked they saw the clouds and the wind as it moved the tree whose branches rested on the roof.

Down Ruby's steps, they walked softly out the front, taking the back way, not past the shore but through the settlement by the old blue-steepled church. He left her at the corner, felt the first drizzle as he watched her go down the street, through the small gate, up the steps and through her door. The sky opened and it poured before he got down the hill.

Past the Busy Bee he saw Redddington's car in front of Noreen's. Under Noreen's awning he lit a cigarette and surveyed the street. Armstrong waved from the cab of his truck as he coasted toward a delivery. Rain came in one thick sheet and stopped as quick as it had come. Somewhere the sun went to work.

"Hello, doll." A hand crept past the sugar and napkins, resting on Noreen's hip.

"Eric Allen! Aren't you the early one."

"Awful, really awful, give me some juice."

Noreen reached under the counter with her back to him, her tight skirt rising.

"Jesus."

She clicked the lever to the little refrigerator.

"The whole bottle?"

"Come on, pour."

He sucked the juice down and brought the cup back to the counter hard, shoving it forward for a refill.

"Where the hell is Reddington?"

"Mama's milking him out back."

"What about me?" he asked, pressing his lips together and kissing the air.

"English?"

"And French. And coffee."

"Noreen." Loud, from the back. "Just what the hell was in that stew for chrissake."

Reddington followed, took a few steps behind the counter, snapping at Noreen's leg with an apron he pulled off a nail where it and some others hung. Noreen mocked a scream and pranced down the aisle on her tiptoes. Reddington took the pancakes, juice, and coffee to the table where Eric sat.

"The stew yesterday was brutal," he said, sitting down. "They had us by the balls up there the other day, where the hell could you go though, Sunday, I mean I told the guy, look, half a buck, but the goddamn glass was like a shot glass. I said bring the cow in for chrissake."

"English."

Eric went to the counter to get the English. Reddington shoved the salt and pepper forward.

"I waited, I don't know, maybe two, three hours."

Eric eyed the English, the butter dripped and rolled down the plate stopping at the French toast.

"An hour I could see, but thirty-five miles up there, then the wait, that's bullshit."

Eric kept his mouth full.

"They'll wait."

"Promises, promises," Noreen said as she scraped the change off the table into the wide pocket of her white apron.

With Reddington it was business as usual but the bar filled the way it had been, drinks held in hands, bodies pushed together formed pockets of flesh, Hannah's flesh had been loose in his hands, as if the skin had been hung loosely on the bones, the room itself damp and hot, when the rain came he had welcomed it. They had run into each other not at the Rose but on the other side, at Mello's Place, and from there had walked the few blocks to the wharves. Past the circle with the flagpole surrounded by white rocks to the other side of the avenue, the gas station, liquor store, all shut. A few motors gargled harbor water. A pair of rubber boots and someone in them faded hollow down the length of the pier. Some fishermen sat by the lobster pots sipping beer.

They lay on the beach, waiting for the lights of
Moore, Counter, or Anthony. Her hair was smooth in
his hand, their bodies warm against each other in the
cool sand. The only one got in was Morrow, drunk,
with scup. The others'd stayed, gone to the North-
ern Edge, by now their cabins were lit, as they were,
one on watch at the wheel, the other two asleep. Key
Marie. Largo. Mary B.

⁓

The houses across the strip of grass around the
bandstand stood staunch, white, their bowels dark.
Captains' wives — Mollys, Sarahs, Rebekahs — had
walked those walks. Steep steps up to the top with
their bonneted heads bent, breaking through with an
arm extended to hold the hatch upright. Sun broke
in, shone off the varnished wainscoting. Weight held
in their forearms passed to the stomach and small of
the back, the other hand used to assist their skirts,
thrust up with the thigh and through to the light to
face what wind there was there. Only some sign, so
little to ask, as they paced the hardwood planks lain

under the white rails, a wish for some meager outline at the end of the endless blue. Meager flowers placed on meager graves where no bones are buried. Lime dispersed into sand churned by undertows, no flow, only those markers a dispatch for the living.

Always some story, some fish story, some sword bigger than anybody'd ever seen, some coast, down south, that winter, the trip down past the Keys, the man lost his hand to the winch. Who'd forget it? The way slack drew and fingers flew through the rolling cable and landed on deck. He remembered them in thick fog. Always lined up on the dock with slime caked on their boots, their long red-and-black caps, thick wool shirts, maroon, checked with aquamarine, deepest black. He ran back and forth with buckets for the baitfish or the tin tubs filled with hooks and line that the old man would hook from the anchor on the back of the truck to a spike on the bulkhead and stretch the length of the parking lot. Father yelled orders from the cab. Son ran frantic, fastened the hooks, did the limbo, his back bent to look. If the line snapped, his head would roll. He'd make up for all his father's errors. Captain Allen. Morgan Allen. He displayed the boy at the gas station, his latest cuts and bruises, the newest plank on the old boat the harbormaster seldom let in the harbor. A navy launch he'd towed past the Bank Towers with a beaten borrowed tug. He beached it in the pond beside some trees, single-handedly broke it up, then put it back together again. No sooner than his new boy could walk, he was put to use. The other brothers had abandoned him, worked on the mainland to support their mother, his daughter, their sister, a paltry excuse. The new boy was his, all his, and he kept him close whenever he could.

Men from the other side by the Creek gathered to watch the boy as he hung off a rope tied to the flying bridge. In and out of the water he went with a hammer in his hand, nails in his mouth and a plank of wood between his feet. Each time he went down the hammer got heavier, the nails harder not to spit or swallow and the plank longer, tougher to move. He got so he could hold a plank with his feet, bend forward rolled into a semi-circle and hammer it in.

If he slipped he fell the length of the slack, the rope grabbed, stopped, and he bounced in midair from the tension. Line gripped under his crotch and shoulders, the pain shooting through his stomach to his neck and throat.

When his father wasn't looking the boy hung there, staring dumb at the rotten green of the hull, trying to figure out how many coats the wreck had on it and how long each new plank would last. The boy scurried around the wharves between the stands set up for drydock like a packrat, kicking and nudging every board he passed. If nothing loose or good enough was on the wharves he'd go to the dump, running down the hill through the burning garbage between the sick old elms armed with bottles to throw at the gulls. He rummaged around until he stacked a pile then found stuff to make a stand for the planks: milk crates, boxes, rocks. Set apart a few feet he'd stack the planks across them then dip his arms under like a forklift. Out of the dirt to the main road that led to the dock he walked the three miles to the water, saw deer as they cut swift through the brush and dead leaves and listened as they smoothly disappeared. By the time the boy was harnessed and dropped from the flying bridge the men from the Creek spotted him and came over. They sat, leaned on the spiles, cheered, laughed, and made bets. The dog was trained to dive off the pier and wrestle the wood away from the boy as he tried to nail it in. Even the father watched with amusement as the dog wrestled the boy over the wood. The dog got better and better and soon knew how to remain underwater long enough to nip at the boy's ankle or thigh. One day the dog took a chunk out of the boy's calf. The men slapped and jostled each other as the boy yelped with hurt. When the dog surfaced the boy hit it over the head with his hammer, grabbed its ear, held its head underwater till he felt its weight stop, release, and the dog sink to the bottom of the harbor. When someone made a motion toward the boy, the boy aimed his hammer at the man's head and said if he took another step he'd do the same to him as he'd done to the dog. They yelled and swore but soon the men dispersed and went back to the other side.

Another day on deck as they worked at baiting tubs the boy asked about the reindeer. Other boys when they gazed from shore thought the signal lights on Bank Towers looked like reindeer. At night over black water, reindeer that flashed red and white. In the sun, the outline of a tail, back and head clear, up front a bright red nose. The father spat at the deck, glared at the boy, kicked tubs in disgust, paced, slapped at the winch handle and muttered. He told him not to go home. To go right from the Fort to the boat and wait in the cabin till he got there. The boy spent the rest of the afternoon in the Fort, in his room, at his table. He stared at his pictures, smoked cigarettes and listened to what the water did to the loose wood underneath. Before the sun went down he walked back to the boat and climbed in the cabin. Through holes in the old wainscoting he could see through to the hull. He heard boats as they docked or left the harbor. Ropes tugged, slack tightened, the boat bobbed with the tide and the spiles creaked.

Steps came back and forth but no body tipped the deck towards the dock with its entering weight. He heard a thud, new weight, and heavy steps on deck. As he went toward the door there was a knock of tin, some tubs tumbled, something dragged and dropped near the door. He pushed at it. Soon the old man's cracked voice sang. A cough, a sputter, the motor turned over and sparked, chugging till it caught and water started to gurgle through the rotten exhaust the boy repaired periodically. It reared, rolled and went ahead. The motor revved then slacked off as the captain navigated the harbor. It died once through the current between the twin jetties, caught till it got loud again and remained that way. He bent his ear to the door to catch a word and heard tubs moved, the winch winding. Every now and then wisps of light filtered through the cracks, runner lights from other boats. Those stopped. He guessed they were out to sea and that his father had shut their own runners off.

The man stumbled to the cabin door, bent to the box he had dragged there and pulled it away. He turned, dragging his feet after him. The door swung open and swayed as if no one had opened it. By the time the boy got used to the little light that came through and stepped toward it, the man was back in the wheelhouse. The Tower's red white signals flashed dead ahead. They stayed straight at them. The boy stood on the steps to the wheelhouse and watched the red white blink on his father's worn out eyes and cragged skin. Once red. Twice white. Twice red. Once white. He popped it in reverse before they would have gone through, let the motor idle, pushed the boy out of the way, went to the rail and grabbed for a piece of frame. The glare of the light through the thick glass fish-eye covers hurt the boy's eyes. The man took the boy by the neck, drew him to his mouth and drawled through the thick liquor breath he'd got from the booze he spent the afternoon drinking: "You want to know the Bank? You want to see fucking reindeer? I'll show you reindeer." With one powerful thrust the man picked the boy up, hoisted him over the railing and deposited him on the tiny square platform one of the pontoons made.

The boy made no sign, looked down, saw where his feet were, clutched the frame and watched his father's mad face stare back. Once red. Twice white. Twice red. Once white. The figure turned from the rail and went back to the wheelhouse. The motor's pitch rose. The boy tried to scream but when he opened his mouth no noise came. With the runners still off the boat slowly faded from the glare of the flashing lights that skimmed across the black water. The noise of the motor disappeared. The only sound left to hide the boy's sobs was the water as it lapped against the pontoons and the bells above him that rang out as the buoys rolled.

RECOLLECTIONS
OF A LATE SPRING

Fish were few and far between though Blunt had claim to a different fortune. The boat was like a quilt, patched together, one year the thing was just too small so Blunt put a bigger hull on it from stuff he picked up at the dump or driftwood. Piece by piece the boat got bigger, each piece different than the next or the last, half of it rotten and held together with wire or spikes. Blunt, his only son a bastard, his daughter inland away from fisheries, from any taint or hint or smell of them, Blunt alone against a purple sky in a bleak year with gulls pecking at bits and scent of bait left on the nets.

A bleak year, his son couldn't imagine how they

107

watched Counter's youngest shrivel slowly from the malnutrition as he walked the docks in the bitter wind hoping to beg a piece of raw fish. He lived with Matt in the farthest shack this side of Eaglet Rock. Even the Indians went hungry, the pass to Mocking Head froze and water was hard to get, it was rabbits mostly kept them going though Billy Kidding Manoot jumped a deer. Like a vulture he waited in a tree must've been nine ten hours when he saw that buck break from his doe he flew and landed on the buck's back, the buck dragged him two three hundred yards through the frozen brush and branches tore Billy Kidding all to shreds before he could slit its throat and wrestle it dead in the snow. The kid got worse and worse. Matt took him out to set traps back of Willows one day and after that the poor scrawny thing could hardly speak so Matt took him in the boat that night and as they went through the channel Matt threw the boy in. He must have caught the rocks then floated through the straights since one of the Indians found him washed up on the beach around the other side of the Head. It was the one called Napoleon who took what was left of him and he and some of the others buried that. The Counters never even went to see where they dug the hole.

⌒

Sand blew across the road. Nap Counter walked from the bulkhead to the gas station kicking pebbles in the air. His hair flew straight ahead of him and covered his ears. He walked past the pumps, opened the door and went into the station. With his one hand he reached into his pocket and put enough change on the counter for some soda and a candy bar. What was left of his other hand hung in a green canvas sling. He had put a big hole through it when his gun jammed hunting duck down by the pond. He didn't stop to talk to Nelly behind the counter but only nodded and walked out the back down past the docks and the fish cutting shed to an old shack that his great grandfather had built.

THE ROAD

He rocked back and forth gently in the seat, bundled up in a coat not thick enough, the collar not high enough to shield his neck from the draft that whistled through the wind lacing, chipped and cracked in places from dry rot. The roads curved dark and came to one-lane covered bridges, perfect S and U turns. He followed smaller rivers until they ended then found the source of them and remained in pursuit, crossing and re-crossing at bridges that looked the longest. The radio crackled then got clear again as he veered in and out of towns whose houses clung to the sides of the mountains, like the road, a ribbon that had been snipped out of the deep-rooted rock and growth. Around a curve he came close to hitting two horses pulling a wagon filled with people. The tires gripped and skidded but he got by them and saw their black figures in the rearview mirror, their arms as they pulled at the reins and the heads of the startled horses whose frothing white teeth gripped their bits and swung a white arc in the black sky as their masters faded back into the black earth. He drove higher and higher, slowing almost to a crawl to peer through the thick banks of fog that had settled over the road. He thought of finding her, if only as a way of explaining that look in her eyes the last time he saw her, when she stepped off the bus and walked across the lot, her legs unsure of her body's weight. He stayed out of the sun watching her until she got in the shadow of a dolly filled with luggage in front of a wall of coin lockers. His eyes must have been wilder, under the moon in the mist, when he had called after her, begging.

The first few months after he met her they had walked through different streets, seeing people she knew or he knew, listening to music or eating or going to the movies. On the 4th of July, they took a train to see her old friends, in a place she had gone to in the summer when her parents were still together. Going back the next day she told him about her first boy, under the house, in the sand. That night, after dinner, they went to her room and she wept into his stomach and fell asleep with her forehead nestled against his ribs. The rest of the summer he and Abe worked on his father's buildings. They painted, plastered, fixed pipes, testified, got judgments, and changed locks. Some of the tenants came back and broke into their old apartments and wrote their names across the walls in spray paint or took hammers and broke up the toilets. They went to the Municipal Building, the hall of records, the housing authority, the welfare bureau, and shuffled through endless files looking for the names on the bells of the buildings and if they had aliases or other addresses and jobs, children, alimony, credit ratings. She danced in the morning and worked in the afternoon. At night he told her who they'd thrown out, who they hadn't, who was coming to repossess the machines in the

Laundromat, whose pipes leaked, whose hot water worked, whose cold water got cut off, whose files they saw, whose number they got. She visited her father and she visited his.

~

He reached a plateau and through the fog saw faint light from a roadhouse. He stopped in a gravel lot overlooking the precipice. Faint laughter and music drifted through the air. He looked at the seat he'd slept in for the last week, stepped out, closed the door and walked up the path to the roadhouse. He had a few drinks then went back to the car. He awoke to a dull thud and a yelp. He cleared his eyes to see a small brown dog chased by a bigger grey one. The sun hadn't yet cleared the top of the mountain. The sky above and to the sides of it remained purple. The one must have cornered the other underneath — there were scrapes, a knock, growls. His coat fell as he got up and leaned over the horn. He tapped it and listened, hearing what must have been the head of the more startled one as it knocked against the chassis, standing in fright. He hit it again, long this time, and heard them, both now, digging at the gravel. They skipped out in front of some logs. The paws of the small brown one scratched at the bumper. His head bobbed up over the chrome flying lady and their eyes met. The other one came up behind him and nudged. They ran over the logs and the gravel, down to a small path and through some hedges. They clawed at the door of the roadhouse but no one answered so they settled there, one on either side of the door, calmly sitting, looking out at the mountain, clear in its outline, the purple drawing back slowly to reveal orange then yellow with china blue behind it. The music and the laughter hadn't given him the glow he'd expected in that clear air. Just the dull, actual thud of movement — brown tables only brown tables, the man's wife his wife, the waitress's black apron faded nylon. The wars his elders had fought were inconceivable, the urgency, misery, and terror of that movement, forests burned, people lined up against walls and shot at random, a defeat so decisive he could only hear the muffled sound of his elbow on the padded vinyl rim of the bar and the words of songs that made him sentimental. Words of songs on jukeboxes whose owners had neglected to keep up to date, words of songs no one could explain the exquisite melancholy of, words he could only hope to mimic the true meaning of:

> In a restless world like this is
> love is ended before it's begun
> and too many moonlight kisses
> seem to cool in the warmth of the sun.

~

Words with pictures clinging to them like barnacles to the numbers corresponding to the days of his life. Old headlines, shoes, shirts, pockets to crowd into, the danger undefined, able to emerge anywhere in speed or violence. And smaller pockets, to be savored, cherished isolation at disparate ends, off lit highways on roads in dark woods or streets whose lights served as beacon not to whom they lit but the light itself as beacon to its own light. Only the light, for a door to open, to be enveloped by the welcome light, welcome me, welcome me to the light welcome light. The china-blue sky certainly a reachable dome, the dogs, eyes of one to the east, eyes of the other to the west, beacons to the unopened door, the day.

Could he get there? Would he even be able to find out where it was he had to get to in order to see her? He could say: Somewhere in Pennsylvania — at least he could say that much to whoever he called if they asked him where he was. Hadn't he been across the street, on the steps of an abandoned building where a man sat drinking a pint of gin, waiting? They had all walked down past the pier, past the boats loading and unloading, getting fuel and checking their oil, to the rocks and across the rocks to the end of the jetty. They sat there and watched a trawler steam through toward the docks. Two men stood on deck, each with a foot on the railing. They waved as the gulls dove and pecked at whatever bait was left on the nets. Would she remember telling him how she had spent the day at the quarries, in the cold deep water, her clothes lying in the moss as she dove off the sides and slid across the sharp black rocks, her body moist on the edge of the soft, damp soil, the leaves above caressed by the breeze?

That was the summer she stayed with him in the small shack near where Abe's brother Jacob lived. He had a small driftwood table, a front page taped above it read: SATCHMO DEAD — A JAZZ ERA ENDS, with a picture of the man, his eyes gazing skyward and a handkerchief drawn up to wipe his watery brow. A few books were wedged in between the wall and an old Hallicrafter shortwave, Hemingway he remembered, and Jack Kerouac. Taped to the top of the Hallicrafter was a clipping from the *Sporting News* with the call numbers and pictures of all the National League announcers. She would drape a shirt over the face plate to keep the mosquitoes away as they lay in bed listening to old band music over Radio Free Europe coming through Germany. At the beach the others sat around the fire while she walked ahead under the moon in the mist, toward the old landing, disappearing behind some rocks. He left the fire and went through the cold sand, toward her, toward the waves that broke over the rocks calling, desperately, as if to claw after her: Will you wait? Will you be there when I get back? Will you wait? I'll always only go a minute. His hands, slow, as if pawing at sheets in the wind, senseless as his brain under the cloud of wine they'd drunk, reaching, to tie her to the rock, to be there, never to move.

～

He pulled into an empty parking lot in front of a boarded-up diner and went to the phone booth at the far end of it. He took all the change out of his pockets, put the coins on the stainless-steel counter and rummaged through his address book and odd slips of paper until he found the number.

He called into it, "Abe?"

Some static broke over the line, the operator came on. He watched some birds on a telephone wire start at the sound of a rig careening down the road. It's spring again, birds on the wing again start to sing that old melody. Say that the birds flew over the diner and were never seen again.

"Abe?"

"Where are you?"

"Somewhere in Pennsylvania. I'm not sure where."

"Are you coming up?"

"I don't know when I'll get there."

"Do you remember how?"

"If I lose myself I'll call you."

The coins dropped and bounced a few times. The change box must have been close to empty. He walked across the lot, shuffling, and watched the gravel and pebbles scatter. Fish swim. Birds fly. Sometimes there's no moon at all. Even lightning bugs dim their lights and stars disappear from sight.

He followed more rivers, went up and down other mountains, across other state lines. He honked the horn as he drove down the narrow dirt road, branches brushing and squeaking against the sides of the wide car. He got to the clearing still honking and could see the white tongue-and-groove door bleached in the sun. Abe stepped out into the yard holding his hand up in greeting. He pulled up in front of the white slat fence that surrounded the garbage cans and the gas canister for the stove.

"It's a beauty." Abe ran his hand across the roof of the long yellow-and-white body.

"I put a transmission in, but other than that," he got out of the car and stretched.

"I'm beat."

They smiled and walked to the front of the car looking at each other. Abe tapped the hood, "bit of a dent," and walked around the passenger side, looking in through the fly window at the gold inscription in cursive on the door of the glove box: Nineteen-Fifty-Six.

"We'll go for a ride later." He looked at the house. He wasn't sure it looked the way it did, or maybe it was that he wanted it to be like the old place. "I never noticed it's like the old place."

"I added that."

"You should have seen this place last night, they were all dancing, some brand of hillbillies I've never seen before, I bought this woman a drink but her husband showed up so I left."

They walked through the woods beyond the clearing, by the fork in the dirt road, down the hill over the stone walls to the pond and then back to the house.

Sam picked up a shirt from the chair before he sat down and held it up: she couldn't have been up to his waist yet.

Abe motioned to a thick catalog on the table. "It's all in there. I tried to get a record once, about a year ago."

"You should come sometime, you wouldn't know anyone."

The sun came in from his back and shone almost all the way across the room. It stopped a foot or so from the wall then began turning orange. The pictures were crooked, there were pictures on the wall above Abe's head and Sam said, "All the pictures are crooked."

Abe turned to look at them and Sam got up and went closer. There was one of them on the running board of one of Sam's old cars. He wore a yellow suit and smoked a cigar. Abe was dressed as King Philip the II, a part he'd played, a young king tattered and torn with old royalty, regally grey and bearded before his time. There was one of Barbara, hiking a football, Abe behind her, their hair flying in the breeze of a cloudy day. There was one of Sam and Jessie and Abe, a small one they'd had taken in one of those machines at the bus station. Abe's head, sideways, took up the bottom, Sam and Jessie above, their chins arched over him. Next to that Abe's father Isaac, grey and wise in a beard in the sun, no hint of court orders, mortgages or speculation deals, warrants, writs, affidavits, cancelled checks and laundry tickets, only unsure in his eyes what the camera meant, why it would want to have something to do with him, why it said now, not then or later. Why this shirt? Why these pants, these shoes? Why this log, this tree to sit on, these leaves, this breeze? Whose sky is this I wait under? Above, clipped to the frame, another one, a card with numbers on it, forty years earlier, his high forehead, deep eyes and black hair, his father's nose, king of the Jews they called him before Pittsburgh got covered in soot, in the service of his country, the country they said was his. Here, take it, serve it: OSS. Below that, Jacob, ten years old, on one knee, with a baseball cap, leaning on a bat in front of a backstop near home plate. From another frame Barbara's perfect eyes met Sam's, the door kicked open and a little voice rose above scattered steps.

"Whose new car, Daddy, whose new yellow car?"

"Uncle's car, Seana, uncle's new yellow car."

Sam swept her off the ground and through the air. "Uncle, uncle," she squealed as he spun her round and round till she landed on the couch. He kissed Barbara, made drinks, and went to the living room to sit next to Seana, her head toward him with her green eyes glinting. He put his hand on her face and told her how it used to cover her whole stomach. He noticed how clean his hand was and tried to remember to a time he had worked with it. He opened the other one, palm first, turning it over and looking in between the fingers and around the nails for grease or paint or scratches or cuts. Seana looked at him and laughed. Abe said, "What are you doing?"

"Look how clean they are." He got up and showed Abe and Abe looked at his. They put them down and sat again, listening to Barbara hum in the kitchen. Seana cocked her head sideways as they all listened to the clack of dishes between the hum.

Sunday morning in the rain Sam could have put her in the palm of his dirty hand. She had tossed and kicked behind the glass, her skin not pink but a deeper hue, almost scarlet. She turned and cried, scratching at her face with her night-old hands and new nails, scratches that took weeks to go away. Abe had picked Sam and Jessie up in front of Sam's building with the old green truck he used to have. They drove through the rain to Renwick Street to make sure the basement of Isaac's paper building hadn't flooded. A building made of mortar and brick and wood and plaster and pipe all on paper. One corporation then another mortgaged it to another on a desk stacked with papers in Isaac's dark one-room apartment. "All filled. What? Can't pay, what do you mean can't pay?" Drag old bones to court, drag young ones in with him, what did the money mean to him? A lousy twenty-four dollars a month paid by a parasite. Or ninety-eight. Or nine hundred, thousand, figures now added, now subtracted, his imagination on fire behind expressionless eyes, all the judges' robes swayed for him and turned to palm trees and a raft somewhere in the sun. The last time Sam saw him they had watched a semi-pro ballgame. They talked about some of the old tenants and he could see the look come back into his eyes. "The best one is where you only give them hot water, that drives them good and crazy. Or when they got a toilet in the hall and you take it out for repairs." The wheels turned and he let out that long silent laugh that ended in a hiss.

Lead Eye who used to just sit by the furnace was gone and Jefferson who threw his stove out the window and took an axe to the walls when his little white lover Joe the shoe salesman broke his heart. Once Abe and Sam were cleaning out the basement and Sam came across Rossoff's stuff, Rossoff who left the building and the sum of his life behind: a few trinkets, a wooden box, some books and two shoeboxes filled with papers, letters and photographs. Out-of-focus pictures of Rossoff with a little girl next to him holding a fish, in some she held it, in others he did, the rod propped against his shoulder on the deck of a green boat. His name wasn't Rossoff but something a lot longer. Sam had given the box to Jessie. It showed a scene of two bears playing in the woods, the sun above them barely breaking through, a stag with its antlers up in the distance eyeing the light blue clouds. On the bottom USSR was carved in bright red. All the other stuff ended up in the dump on Gansevoort Street where men with canvas bags waded waist deep in garbage below the fumes and stink for the prize of some pot-metal or forgotten coin.

They had set the pump to work on the rain-water and strung the cord precariously up out of the basement, through the halls and up the stairs above the toilet in the second floor hall to a light fixture replaced by a combination socket that shook when the toilet gurgled. They drove over the edge of the island on the bridge to the Navy Yard where Isaac's super was being held prisoner at the Federal House of Detention for being an illegal alien but they were early so the guard tried to elicit a bribe. Instead of taking the bait, they turned and went back over the bridge and uptown through the rain and the traffic that had both gotten heavier to the maternity ward where Sam gave Barbara a bunch of flowers Jessie had picked at a florist on Seventh Avenue. Barbara lay under the sheets drugged, her eyes bright with a silly smile as she watched Abe and Sam.

Soon after that Abe, Barbara, Seana, and even Isaac moved to the country. Jessie too moved with her father who went from place to place. She came back every now and then but that stopped. Sam wrote to her every now and then, but that stopped too. The letters he got back were mostly about her mother though what she didn't write seemed to be about her father. When she had seen Sam with his father it made her jealous but she kept it to herself, not wanting to remember when her father left, how she had run back and forth between him and her mother, tugging at their clothes. Even so she stayed close to her father and Sam never thought that staying close to him had much to do with her mother doing herself in. Everyone knew it was coming, Jessie more than anyone, and the loss was almost a relief. She'd seen hope waste too many people around her so she stood that way, eyes up against them while she polished her own secret jewel for fear it might shatter and break, losing all its glint, to scatter in shards along the flat, common ground. She tolerated her father's distance as it was that much less the remove she kept with others. Abe dug his foundations deep while Jacob and Sam had things to do: there was this to do, that to do, this, and that too, and the temptation became overwhelming to reduce everything to the chicken and the egg, the egg and the suspenders, the chicken and the road.

Seana had gone to bed. Abe and Barbara drank in the living room. Sam sat by the phone and rummaged through the old book dialing numbers he hadn't dialed in a long time. From one lead to another he got an address in Canada. Jessie was there, with friends of the family, the phone they weren't sure of. He finally got it through information. An operator came on, faint, in broken English and French Canadian, it was one of those private phone companies. She rang up and a man answered through the static,

politely, calmly. He said to hold the line, that Jessie
had difficulty in walking and was in another part of
the house. He waited listening to Abe and Barbara
talking, going silent, then talking again.

"We tried there too."

Sam stretched the cord as far as he could get from
the doorway, going toward the window. She spoke
again. "I lost forty pounds, months and months with
tubes and wires."

Something in his stomach dropped. He jerked
dumbly at the window as he listened. "I must have
been somewhere," he said, " I mean I must not have
been where I usually am, like now, here, where I am
now, which isn't usually where I am." He thought
of Jacob gone and wanted to remember some lines
in Spanish that he loved, the thought of them sung
with feet stamping in a release of joy so hard it got
bitter with the lines spat out but he only remembered one, the last one: "Hasta cuando partamos,
despidámonos!"

The taste was still with him in the morning,
somewhere between his tongue and his throat. He

ate the toast Abe made and guzzled a glass of juice Barbara had squeezed. Abe sat to his eggs. Seana looked at Sam and at her food without eating it. It was earlier for her than usual. She got up and stood behind her chair.

"I'll send a check," Sam told Abe. He looked at Seana but she just turned and stared at the seat of the chair. "No rush," he said and motioned in the air with his fork. Barbara came up behind her, put her hand on her daughter's head and softly asked her to eat.

On the way out he didn't honk but the branches still brushed against the sides of the wide car. He stopped at the end of the dirt road to take a look at the map he had in the glove compartment. There was a ways to go till the border. Continuing across, he took that desolate stretch of road further north: squat wire fences with grey posts and faded signs on rusted mounts, a vast intractable land under an un-changing sky. He drove by what he knew must be the house, slow wide hills, then flat for a stretch, all grey, the houses weathered grey, the shingles tight and straight. He pulled off to the dirt shoulder and left it there, the faded lines disappearing in the distance. He got to the short path leading to the house and heard a screen door creak as a woman wearing a white cotton dress emerged from the shadow. Before he said anything, she started: "You've just missed her, we tried to call, the one that answered said you had left. She's gone to meet her father, my husband drove her." He watched her small lips, her handsome face below her grey hair, the lines belonging there. He nodded, as the voice came back to him again, through the static, after all the waiting: "Ten, twelve, fifteen times, my stomach, my back, my legs, my arms. It was complicated. Believe me I tried." He imagined her lying on the sidewalk in a pool of blood soaked black into the cement. The knife was found in a trashcan. He thanked her again and said goodbye, hearing the door snap back and her steps fade through the hall of the empty house. Listening to their echo, he turned to look at the vast flat land below the thick grey sky.

ABOUT THE AUTHOR

Ammiel Alcalay is poet, translator, critic, and scholar who teaches at Queens College and the CUNY Graduate Center. He is the author of, among other books, *After Jews and Arabs* (1993); *the cairo notebooks* (1993); *Memories of Our Future* (1999); *from the warring factions* (2002); *and Scrapmetal* (2007). A new book of essays, *A Little History*, is due out in 2010. He was one of the initiators of the *Poetry Is News Coalition*, and helped to organize the *Olson Now* project. He has recently launched *Lost & Found: The CUNY Poetics Document Initiative*, a publishing venture whose mission is to retrieve and make available key texts falling widely under the rubric of the New American Poetry.